This P.B. Bear book belongs to

JULIA & JILLIAN

WITH LOTS OF LOVE
NANNA
TENNANT

Pyjama Bedtime Bear   **Milly**   **Russell**   **Dermott**

door   postcard   aeroplane   shorts   shirt

thermos   backpack   sunglasses   binoculars   boat

parrot   crocodiles   spiders   frogs   butterflies

hummingbirds   lizards   snakes   tree   sandwiches

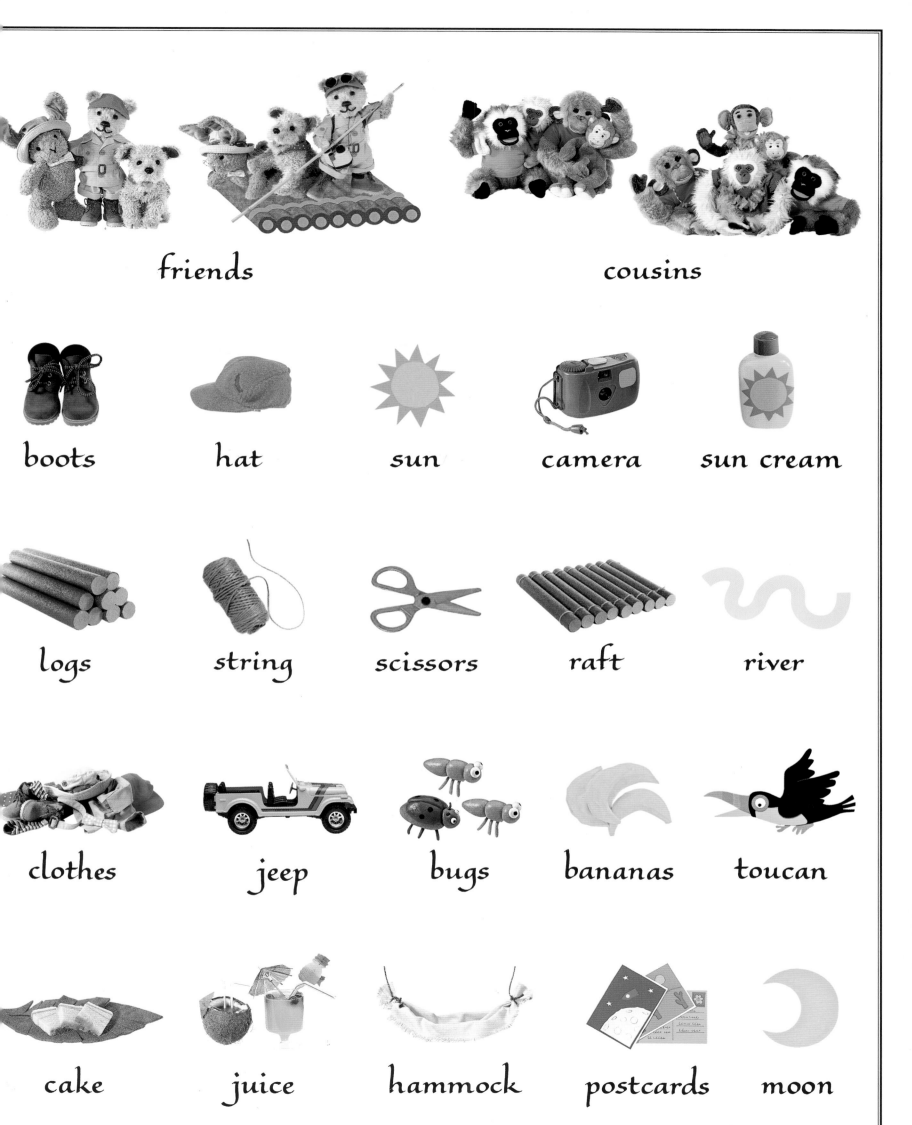

friends

cousins

boots

hat

sun

camera

sun cream

logs

string

scissors

raft

river

clothes

jeep

bugs

bananas

toucan

cake

juice

hammock

postcards

moon

www.dk.com

Designers Chris Fraser, Claire Jones, Lisa Hollis
Editors Bridget Gibbs, Fiona Munro
DTP Designer Jill Bunyan
Photography Dave King
Illustration Judith Moffatt
Production Joanne Rooke

First published in Great Britain in 1999 by Dorling Kindersley Limited,
9 Henrietta Street, London WC2E 8PS

ISBN 0-7513-7162-9

Colour reproduction by Colourscan
Printed and bound in Italy by L.E.G.O

A CIP catalogue record for this book is
available from the British Library.

Acknowledgments
Dorling Kindersley would like to thank the following manufacturers
for permission to photograph copyright material:
Ty Inc. for "Toffee" the dog.
The Manhattan Toy Company for "Antique Rabbit".
Merrythought Ltd. for Postman Monkey.
John Lewis Ltd. for black-faced monkey.
Dowman Imports Ltd. for "Gibbon".

Dorling Kindersley would also like to thank the following people
for their help in producing this book:
Maggie Haden, Richard Blakey, Vera Jones, Steve Gorton and Stephen Raw.

Can you find the little bear
in each scene?

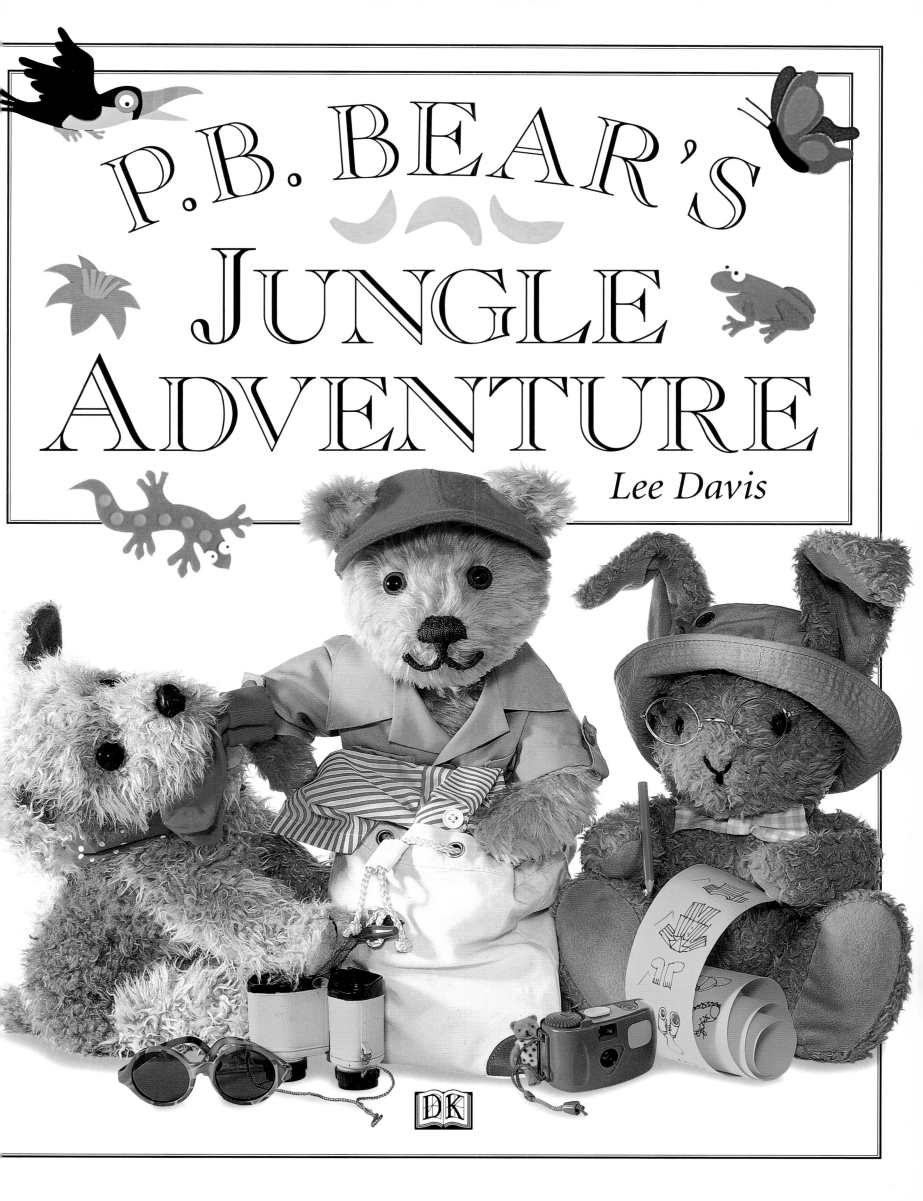

P.B. BEAR'S
JUNGLE
ADVENTURE

Lee Davis

One day the postman knocked at P.B. Bear's  .

"Good morning! Here's a for you," he said.

"It looks like it's from your friend Milly  ."

"It is," said P.B. Bear  .

"She's in the jungle visiting her cousins. She wants us to go and meet them."

"But how will we get there? The jungle is a long way from here," said Russell 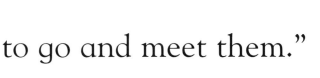 .

"We'll have to take an for a start," said P.B.

"Then we'll find a way up the river into the rainforest."

P.B. put the 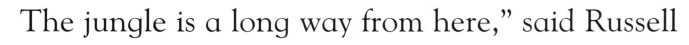 in his postcard album.

"Now, let's pack our bags," he said.

"Wow! A jungle adventure!" said

Dermott  . "Let's go!"

Dear P.B. and friends
I'm staying with my cousins in the jungle for the holidays. Please come and visit. We'll have a party! You'll find us near the end of the river.

Love, Milly

PS The jungle is hot, steamy and busy!

Mr Pyjama B. Bear
9 Henrietta Street
Covent Garden
London. WC2

P.B. found his jungle  ,

and some sturdy  . He put on a

red  to keep off the  .

He packed his  , a bottle

of  , and a  in his  .

He got his  and his  , then the friends boarded

their  and flew off

to the rainforest.

When the  got off the plane they walked to the river. "Now what?" asked . "We haven't got a ."

"We're brave explorers," said P.B. Bear. "We'll make a raft. There are plenty of we can use. Let's collect them."

"I packed some thick and !" said Dermott.

At last, the was ready.

"Off we go!" said .

The [raft] went up the [river], deep into the rainforest. There were animals in the trees, [4] and 5 [fish], "What's that hissing noise?" asked [dog].

on the ground and in the river. Can you spot 1, 2, 3,

Soon they came to a deep pool below a beautiful waterfall. The  were very hot, so they threw off their and jumped in.

When they had cooled off,

they climbed out of the water and

got dressed again. "Where are we?"

asked   , looking around.

"I've got a map," said   ,

"but there's no waterfall shown on it.

I think we're a little bit lost."

"Will we ever get there?" asked  .

"I wish we had a fast  ."

Just then, the  heard a voice,

"Follow the bananas, follow the bananas."

They looked around and saw a  in the trees.

"Look," said  , "there's a trail of bananas."

"The  know the way!" said P.B. Bear.

"Follow the  , follow the  ,"

the friendly  squawked again.

So they did.

The friends followed the banana trail through the jungle.

They saw a big and some little  . They saw

quick  and slithery . And they saw lots

of . Suddenly, they heard someone call "Help!"

The  looked up.

The sound was coming

from the top of a tall .

"Help, I'm stuck!"

"It's a baby monkey!" said  .

"Maybe it's one of Milly's cousins 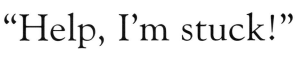 ." Suddenly

there were monkeys everywhere, all rushing to help.

"There's  !" said  .

"Let's see if we can help!"

The monkeys and the

climbed the tree, which

soon started to sway.

"It looks a bit wobbly,"

said  .

"Watch out!" shouted  .

But it was too late. There was a big **CRASH!**

All the monkeys came tumbling down and landed in a heap.

"Welcome!" said . She introduced her  to her  as they all picked themselves off the ground.

Just then the  squawked, "Follow the  ! Follow the  !" and everyone started laughing.

"Now it's time to party!" said  .

and her  organised a jolly jungle party!

All the  joined in.

Everyone ate  and and lots of .

They drank delicious and danced until

the went down.

Before settling down in his  to sleep,  wrote  by the light of the  to his friends at home. Then he fell asleep and dreamed of the jungle.

P.B. Bear loves to look at photos to remind him of his adventures. These are some of his favourites.
Where would you like to go on holiday?